MICE TWICE

By The Same Author

Boo to a Goose
The Christmas Grump
What If...?

(MARGARET K. MCELDERRY BOOKS)

Mice Twice

story & pictures by JOSEPH LOW

A MARGARET K. MCELDERRY BOOK

Atheneum 1983 *New York*

For a Particular Mouse

Library of Congress Cataloging in Publication Data

Low, Joseph.
  Mice twice.
  "A Margaret K. McElderry book."
  SUMMARY: A round of uneasy hospitality results when
Mouse and Dog arrive at Cat's house for dinner.
  [1. Animals—Fiction] I. Title.
PZ7.L9598Mi   [E]   79-23274
ISBN 0-689-50157-9

Published simultaneously in Canada by McClelland & Stewart, Ltd.
Printed by Connecticut Printers, Inc., Hartford
Bound by A. Horowitz & Son/Bookbinders
Fairfield, New Jersey
First Printing July 1980
Second Printing May 1981
Third Printing November 1981
Fourth Printing November 1983

CAT was thinking about supper.
He thought, "I could eat forty-seven grasshoppers.
Or I could eat sixty-nine crickets.
Or I could eat a fine, fat sparrow.
But what I think I'd *really* like
is a nice, tender mouse."

So he went and sat outside Mouse's door.
"Are you there, Mouse," he asked, "and
in good health, I hope?"

Mouse lay snug in her nest behind the door.
The door was too small for Cat to get through.

"Never better," she said.

Cat tuned his rough voice to make it smooth.
He said, "Such a lovely day! I was just thinking,
'How nice to have a friend for supper.'
I do hope you can join me this evening."

Mouse knew Cat well, and all his cunning ways.
"May I bring a friend?" she asked.

("Mice twice!" thought Cat, licking his whiskers.)
"By all means," he said. "Shall we say six o'clock?"

"Six will be fine," said Mouse.

At six that evening she knocked on Cat's door.
Cat's stomach rumbled. "Come in, come in!" he said.
But when he opened the door, he saw that
Mouse's friend was not another mouse.

It was Dog. Dog was grinning.
He was twice as big as Cat.

Cat was angry, but he was afraid to show it.
He waved them into the house.
On the table were two small bits of cheese.

"Such a warm day!" said Cat. "I find it best not to eat on warm days. But do help yourselves."

So Mouse took one piece of cheese.
And Dog took the other.

When he had swallowed his, Dog said, "I have
seldom enjoyed a cheese so much. Is it Swiss?"

"Or is it French?" asked Mouse.

"French," said Cat. "A gift from my cousin Pierre."

(Actually, it was common old rat-trap cheese,
as Dog and Mouse knew very well.)

Dog said, "It has been so pleasant, dear Cat.
I hope you will have dinner with me tomorrow night."
Cat thought for a moment. "I will, indeed," he
said, "if I may bring a friend."
"Good company makes for good eating," said Dog.
"Bring any friend you like. Shall we say
seven o'clock?"
"Seven will be fine," said Cat.

At seven the next night, Cat knocked on Dog's
door. Beside him stood Wolf – twice as big
as Dog. Four times as fierce.
"Come in, come in!" called Dog.

Cat looked at Wolf. He whispered, "Dog for you.
Mouse for me. Agreed?"
Wolf said nothing, but curled his lip in a
horrid smile. All his sharp teeth were showing.
Cat and Wolf both licked their whiskers.

But when the door opened,
there beside Dog sat Crocodile.
His big, toothy jaws slowly opened and closed
as he smiled at Cat and Wolf.

Cat and Wolf stared at that gaping mouth. So big!
So red! So many, many teeth! They could not
take their eyes away. Not even to look at
the four pieces of cheese on the table.

"Ummmm," said Wolf,
looking over his shoulder
at the door.

"Actually," said Cat, "we came to ask if we might
make it another night. Neither of us is feeling well."
"What a pity!" said Dog. "I had so hoped you
might enjoy this delicate French cheese.
Brie, it is called."

(And it really *was* French Brie.)

"Another time," mumbled Cat as he and Wolf
backed out the door.

Cat thought for a moment, looking back at
Crocodile. "Tomorrow night," he said, "I'd like you
to meet a distant relative who will be visiting me
for dinner. Can you join me – and bring your friend?"

"Delighted," said Dog.

"But not Crocky, here.
He must get back to the river tonight. Perhaps
Mouse might come, if that is agreeable?"

"Splendid!" said Cat, trying not to grin. "I will
expect you at eight o'clock."

At eight the next evening Dog and Mouse
knocked on Cat's door.

Inside sat Lion, so big he all but filled the
house. Cat had to sit between his huge paws.
Cat was smiling.

In the space remaining at one side was a table.
It was covered with dishes of good things Cat had
bought to please Lion. There were fresh-roasted
peanuts; fat, juicy raisins; little cakes covered
with sugar frosting; bits of fried and crumbled
bacon; and a silver tray of mint candies.

Cat looked up and whispered to Lion,
"When the door opens, I will grab Mouse,
you grab Dog, and that will be that!"
"That!" rumbled Lion, licking his whiskers
with his rough, red tongue.

"How prompt you are!
Come in! Come in!"
cried Cat to Dog.

As the door swung open,
both Cat and Lion leaned forward,
their mouths already open.

Neither of them had noticed that Dog and Mouse
had brought their good friend, Wasp.

Quick as a wink, Wasp stung Lion's nose.
Then his ear. Then his rough, red tongue.
Lion was frantic!

He tried to back away, but Cat's house was
too tight around him.

Wasp stung his lip.

Lion broke the house apart and ran.

Cat ran after him.

And Dog after Cat.

Cat's house was wrecked, but the table was unharmed.

All the good things on it
stood as they had been.

"Good friend," said Mouse to Wasp, "do help yourself
to anything you fancy. Those little cakes, perhaps?
Or one of the mints? I rather like the smell of
those peanuts, myself, for starters. Plenty here
for both of us, and a good share, too, for Dog,
if Cat escapes what he deserves."

If Cat *did* escape, you may be sure he never
bothered Mouse again.

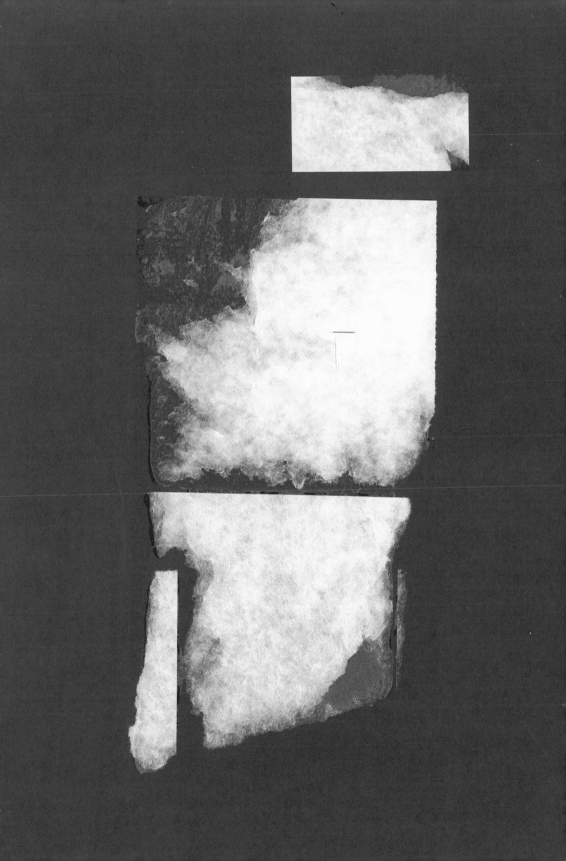

Enchantment of America

Panoramic Plains

THE GREAT PLAINS STATES

Iowa • Kansas • Missouri • Nebraska
North Dakota • South Dakota

By Frances E. Wood
Illustrated by Ed Morgan

CHILDRENS PRESS • CHICAGO

Educational Consultant for the

Enchantment of America Series:

Marilyn M. Spore, Laboratory School,

University of Chicago

Regional Consultant for PANORAMIC PLAINS:

Keith Huntress, Ph.D.,

Professor of English and Speech,

Iowa State University

Library of Congress Catalog Card Number: 62-9075

Copyright, 1962, Childrens Press
Printed in the U.S.A.

7 8 9 10 11 12 13 14 15 16 17 18 19 20 21 22 23 24 25   R   75 74 73 72

Contents

The Land—prehistory to present

Location

The eastern section of the Plains States is usually considered a part of the Central Plains, while the western section forms a part of the Great Plains, or High Plains. The states of this region—Missouri, Iowa, North Dakota, South Dakota, Nebraska, Kansas—lie between the Middlewestern States on the east and the Rocky Mountain and Plateau States on the west, with Canada on the north. Each of these states played a colorful role in the history of our country, and each has its own individual claim to scenic beauty, fertile soil, and fine living conditions.

Land and Life from Beneath the Sea

The vast plains are a part of the interior lowlands of America. Several hundred million years ago they were largely covered by a shallow inland sea. At first there was practically no life in this sea. Then tiny plants appeared, and animals, including animals with shells. As thousands upon thousands of years passed, these animals and plants became larger and larger. Some of the animals crawled about the bottom of the sea or burrowed through the slimy mud. Fish swam in the water.

Slowly the land rose above the shallow sea, and then as slowly sank again and was once more covered by the sea. This happened many times, and each time that the sea returned and covered the land, new layers of mud and sand and crushed sea shells were left on the bottom. These materials that were laid down by ancient seas became sedimentary rocks. Fossils of ancient sea animals and plants are often found in them. The crushed sea shells were the beginning of the limestone that lies beneath most of the Plains region today.

For millions of years, fish and shelled animals and other sea animals were the only creatures in the world. Then amphibians, four-legged animals which can live both in water and on the land, began to develop. Huge frogs and giant salamanders and many other strange creatures lived in and out of the water. Some were small animals that could climb trees; others were as long as alligators and lived in swamps. Giant dragonflies, enormous cockroaches, and other insects flew about in the air or crawled on the ground.

Each time the sea withdrew, jungles of giant ferns and other plants grew in the marshes and bogs that were left behind. And each time it returned, the plants were buried under water and heavy layers of mud and sand. The weight of these sediments compressed the decaying plants into beds of black rock, or coal. The outlines of the leaves of plants that remain as fossils in much of the coal today tell how it was formed.

Millions of years rolled by. Egg-laying reptiles of many kinds appeared. Some lived on land, some in the water, and some could live on both land and water. Some could even fly. A winged reptile that lived in what is now Kansas had a wingspread of nearly thirty feet, a body that weighed twenty-five pounds, and a beak three feet long.

Giant turtles, twelve feet and more in length and weighing 6,000 pounds, inhabited the shallow sea that once again covered the Plains region. By this time, the sea teemed with life—large and small fish and strange-looking marine lizards and other reptiles. The remains of fish thirty feet long and queer-looking reptiles fifty feet long have been found in Kansas.

As the sea subsided, leaving lakes and marshes and bogs, dinosaurs appeared. The first ones were small; then much larger ones developed —huge monsters that ruled both the land and the water and fought among themselves. These were reptiles, too, and they looked even stranger than the ones that had gone before them.

11

The Coming of Mammals

As the dinosaurs disappeared, warm-blooded mammals developed. Most of these were covered with hair and bore their young alive instead of hatching them from eggs. Some of these mammals would look very strange to us, but others were quite similar to our present-day mammals.

About sixty million years ago, the sea withdrew for the last time from the interior of North America, and warm-blooded animals became common and spread throughout the land. As the climate became cooler, the marshes dried up, and mountain building began in the west. Grass grew on the plains, and the land began to look much as it does today.

Herds of hoofed animals grazed on the plains—small horses, some with one toe and some with three; short-legged, chunky rhinoceroses; large peccaries, with long faces and bumps on their cheeks; camels, with long, slim legs and long necks, like giraffes. Along with these were four-toed mammals that looked a little like sheep and a little like pigs, and many different kinds of deer-like animals, with two or three or more horns that grew in various places on their heads. Preying upon these grass-eating mammals were the saber-toothed cats, gigantic dogs, and smaller wolves, dogs, weasels, and other flesh-eating animals.

12

The Age of Ice

About one million years ago, a strange thing began happening to the northern part of North America. The climate became colder and colder until there was scarcely any summer at all. So much snow fell in the north that it could not melt, and a great ice sheet was formed, a mile or more thick, which began moving because of its own weight. Slowly it moved down through Canada into what is now the interior of the United States and covered that part of the Plains region that is north and east of the Missouri River. As the ice sheet moved down across the continent, it scraped up rocks and soil and carried them along. It smoothed the surface of the land. When the ice sheet melted, it left behind great quantities of fertile soil.

Four or five times the ice sheet advanced into central North America and then, as the climate warmed again, it melted back into the North. Each time it brought more black, rich soil to the plains.

During the long intervals between the coming of the ice sheets, plants flourished and animals ranged the plains. Each time the ice sheet moved down across the continent, it covered the plants and forced the animals southward. But the more hardy ones, like the musk ox and the caribou and moose, stayed to graze along the edge of the ice sheet. Each time, as it melted back, the animals moved northward with it. Some of these animals developed in North America; others, such as the bison and the mammoth and mastodon, came to this continent over a land or ice bridge between Alaska and Siberia.

By the end of the Ice Age, many animals had disappeared entirely. The horse became extinct in North America and did not reappear until it was introduced by the Spaniards thousands of years later. The rhinoceros, camel, saber-toothed cat, and many others were gone from this continent forever. The mammoths and mastodons probably lingered on for a few thousand years after the last ice sheet had melted from the interior of the United States but they, too, were soon gone. Other animals remained and became the ancestors of those we know today.

The Land of the Plains States Today

There is a great variety of land forms in the Plains States—glaciated prairies and high western plains; rolling hills, deep river valleys, and low, but rugged, mountains; tablelands and ancient lake beds; fantastic "badlands."

From time to time, glaciers covered all of Iowa, the northern part of Missouri, only the extreme northeast corner of Kansas and a narrow strip in eastern Nebraska, about half of South Dakota, and almost all of North Dakota. Today most of these areas are covered by a deep, rich soil deposited by the receding glaciers thousands of years ago.

Another type of soil, called "loess," is found in the Plains States. Loess was formed when fine mud along the edge of glaciers dried into dust, and was caught up by the wind and deposited in other areas. A good place to see it is in the brownish-colored dust cliffs and bluffs along the Missouri River between Iowa and Nebraska.

The soil in the western section of the Plains States, and the layers of rock underneath, were not deposited by glaciers. These materials were laid down by ancient seas that once covered the area. More soil was added later when ancient mountains that lay to the west were worn down. The soil was thickest near the base of the old mountains and spread out thinner and thinner toward the east. That is why today the plains slope from an altitude of several thousand feet on the west to a few hundred feet on the east.

The land of the Plains States is generally flat or gently rolling, with some exceptions. Only one ice sheet covered the northeast corner of Iowa, and that is a rugged, scenic area known locally as "Little Switzerland." High bluffs border many of the rivers, and those along the Mississippi and the Missouri are especially beautiful. Toward the west, small hills, buttes, and pinnacles rise above the surrounding plains. The low Ozark Mountains are in southern Missouri. In the Dakotas are badlands, which have been carved into fantastic shapes by the rivers and rains of the area. The Black Hills, with the highest peaks east of the Rocky Mountains, are in South Dakota, and the Turtle Mountains, about 2,000 feet high, are on the border between North Dakota and Canada.

The Red River of the North and the Mississippi River form most

of the eastern boundary of the Plains States. The Missouri River, longest in the United States, courses through, or touches on, all of the states. The Missouri flows into the Mississippi at St. Louis, and the two rivers taken together make one of the longest rivers in the world. The Red River of the North forms the border between North Dakota and Minnesota and then flows north to Lake Winnipeg in Canada. The wide, fertile valley of this river was once the bed of a huge ancient lake, of which Lake Winnipeg and Lake of the Woods are remnants.

There are numerous small natural lakes and pot-holes in the glaciated areas, but most of the large lakes are man made. They were built for flood-control and irrigation purposes, as well as for electric power and recreation. In the southern area, especially Missouri, are many natural springs and limestone caves.

When we are traveling on the plains, the road usually rolls out ahead of us in a straight east-west or north-south direction. If we look down on the area from an airplane, we can see that the farms are laid out in neat rectangles or squares. All of this is because, when the land was first opened to settlement, the government divided it into sections one mile square, with roads between. These sections could then be divided into half or quarter sections for people who wanted less land, but the sides were kept straight.

Climate

Although it differs somewhat from east to west and north to south, the states of the Plains region have what we call a "continental" climate. This is the sort of climate, with hot summers and cold winters, that is usually found in the interior of a continent which is separated by mountains from the oceans and their moderating effects.

The northern section of the Plains region has long, very cold winters, with heavy snowfalls and frequent blizzards. The summers are humid and warm. The winters in the southern section are not quite so cold, and the long summers are hot and humid. The states in this area produce fine corn, which needs humid weather and a long growing season.

The western section of the Plains region—that is, the High Plains —is much drier than the eastern section. The High Plains are semi-arid. Fierce blizzards roar across them in the wintertime and sometimes bring death to great numbers of cattle and sheep. In the summer, tornadoes and destructive hail are not infrequent. Kansas and Iowa have more tornadoes than any other states, and more than any other comparable areas in the world.

Things to think about

Describe the progress of the inland sea and its effect on the land.

What effects did the Ice Age have on this region?

What are the different soils in the Plains region? What caused the variety?

What is the general elevation and "lay of the land" today?

Describe the "continental" climate of the Plains States.

19

People come to the plains

The First People

We tend to think of Leif Ericson and Christopher Columbus as the discoverers of America, but, in reality, the New World had been discovered about 25,000 years before that, by people coming from the opposite direction. Sometime during the latter part of the Ice Age they crossed the Bering Strait by means of the fifty-mile land or ice bridge that once connected America and Siberia.

The first to cross over were probably a small band of hunters, perhaps a man and his family, who had followed a herd of bison or mammoths across the bridge. There was little ice in Alaska at this time, and the hunters found many animals feeding on the lush, green grass. No doubt more families soon followed, until many people were coming. Little by little, some of them made their way across the mountains to areas which the ice sheet had not reached. Some stayed in the plains area, while others moved south to warmer climes. With them were their faithful dogs, the only animal that man had domesticated at this time.

By the end of the Ice Age, or shortly thereafter, many of the big-game animals had disappeared from the North American continent. The mammoths and giant bison that the hunters had followed into the New World were gone; so were the horses, camels, giant beavers, and many other animals. The hunting was not so good now, and the people had to live on small game and on nuts and roots and berries.

For the thousands of years between the end of the Ice Age and the beginning of the farming era, little is known about the Indians of the Great Plains. There were few cliffs or caves or other means of preserving the habitations of these prehistoric Indians, and the Mound Builders had penetrated only into the extreme eastern section.

It is believed that the Mound Builders entered the Mississippi Valley about 2,000 years before the birth of Christ and spread over the eastern half of the United States. Thousands of their earthen mounds are found in the Mississippi and Ohio valleys and in other parts of the East. Some of these mounds are pyramidal in shape, with flat tops, on which wooden temples once stood. Others were burial mounds, often in the form of birds or other animals. The mounds preserved in the Effigy Mounds National Monument, which is near the west bank of the Mississippi River in northeastern Iowa, are some of the most outstanding of these.

The First Farmers of the Plains

When excavations were started some years ago to build the great man-made lakes along the Missouri River, the remains of hundreds of prehistoric Indian villages were found beneath layers of earth. Scientists were called in by the excavators to preserve as many of the relics as possible and to trace the story of the villages. When the scientists examined the village sites and relics laid bare by the excavating shovels, they discovered that a race of farming people had once lived throughout the Great Plains.

These people lived in houses made of wooden poles, bark, and earth. Some of the houses were round and some square, and they were sunk a foot or more into the earth. At some sites were fortifications, showing that warfare was going on between some tribes. Among the household relics were different kinds of pottery, made by different tribes, and farm implements made from stone and the bones of animals. Smoking pipes were found, too, for these Indians raised tobacco, as well as corn, beans, and squash.

The Indians obtained meat and skins for clothing, bedding, and tepees by hunting elk, deer, antelope, buffalo, and other animals. The buffalo, which were really smaller versions of the great bison that had entered North America from Siberia during the Ice Age, roamed the western plains in large herds. During the season that the herds moved closest to the Indian villages, the hunting parties went out to meet them, to obtain the year's supply of buffalo meat.

22

Horses were unknown to the Indians at this time, and they traveled on foot and used dogs to pull their small *travois*. The front ends of the travois poles were fastened to the shoulders of dogs, and the rear ends dragged on the ground. The skins for the tepees and other household effects were lashed to the poles, which were also used for the tepees when the Indians made camp.

The women led the dogs and usually carried light packs on their backs. The men were left free to hunt buffalo and to ward off hostile Indians and other dangers. Hunting buffalo afoot, with spear or bow and arrow, was a difficult and dangerous task, and the hunters needed their full attention for it. After the kill, the women prepared some of the meat to be eaten immediately, and some of it was cut in long strips and dried, for use during the long winter months ahead.

Horses

Before most of the Plains Indians had even seen a white man, his coming to the New World brought a change that was to affect their whole way of living. This was the introduction of horses into the New World. Before becoming extinct in America during the Ice Age, some of these animals had migrated to Siberia by way of the land or ice bridge across Bering Strait. They had spread all over Asia and Europe, where the people had eventually domesticated them and used them for beasts of burden. The Spaniards, on their exploring expeditions, brought horses back to America, and some of them got loose and became wild. Within the next hundred years, horses had again spread throughout the Southwest and into the Plains areas. And it did not take the Indians very long to learn to catch them and break them to ride and carry burdens.

25

By the time white settlers reached the Plains, horses had completely changed the life of the Plains Indians. Now they were able to ride much faster than they had been able to walk, and for longer distances, and they became swift hunters and mighty warriors. The horses were able, too, to drag much heavier travois, with longer poles, so that the Indians were able to take larger, more comfortable tepees with them. Gradually, the Plains Indians turned from an agricultural way of living to a nomad life, following the buffalo herds as they moved from place to place. Only a few Indians remained in villages and tilled their fields of corn and squash and beans. Horses became so important to the Plains Indians that they were used for barter, much as we use money today.

Coronado Comes to the Plains

After Columbus had discovered the New World and claimed it for Spain, Spaniards began exploring the southern end of North America, and entered what is now the United States from Mexico. Coronado, one of the Spanish explorers, traveled north in search of legendary cities of gold that he had heard the Southwest Indians talk about, and he entered what is now Kansas in 1541. But Coronado did not find his golden cities, and he soon left the plains in disgust.

The French Claim the Land.

The next white men to visit the area were French explorers and missionaries. Father Marquette, Louis Jolliet, and Robert La Salle traveled the Great Lakes and down the Mississippi River. Soon all the land on both sides of the river was claimed for the French king, and forts were built east of the river.

Missionaries and fur traders penetrated the land to the west, largely by means of the Missouri River and other streams. The town of Ste. Genevieve was founded on the west bank of the Mississippi about 1635 by lead miners.

But it was not until 1738 that Pierre de la Vérendrye explored for France the country that is now North Dakota. Later, his sons explored South Dakota.

The land east of the Mississippi was ceded to the English at the end of the French and Indian War, who in turn ceded it to the Americans at the end of the Revolutionary War. France had given the land west of the river and New Orleans, at its mouth, to Spain, but Napoleon forced Spain to return the territory to France.

The Louisiana Purchase

In 1803 Napoleon, hard pressed by war in Europe, sold all of this land, including New Orleans, to the United States for fifteen million dollars. This was known as the Louisiana Purchase and included most of the area that is now the Plains States.

The coming of the white man changed the lives of the Indians. The white settlers in the east crowded the eastern Indians farther west, and they, in turn, armed with the white man's guns and knives, pushed their neighboring tribes still farther west. The Chippewas, with guns obtained from the French, pushed the farming Dakotas and the Cheyennes onto the plains.

Lodges and Tepees of the Plains People

French and, later, American explorers found the Mandans, Hidatsas, and Pawnees still living in earth lodges. These lodges were so well made that early settlers on the plains built their own sod houses in much the same way.

A strong wooden framework formed the walls and a dome-shaped roof. Except for a hole in the center of the roof to let out smoke, all the framework was first covered with branches, then grass and sod, and then earth. This made a warm, snug dwelling that shut out the winter cold and driving snow. Usually the floor was dug down to a depth of a foot or more and the walls were set back from the edge far enough to leave an earthen bench clear around the lodge, a very handy place on which to sit or to store household articles. Many of the lodges had entryways which further shut out the cold.

The Mandans and Hidatsas kept their round bull-boats, made of wooden frames and buffalo skins, on the roofs of the lodges and turned them over the smoke-holes in bad weather. Hunting trophies and other objects were also displayed on the roofs, which were strong enough for people to sit on.

A different type of house was built by the Caddoan tribes. The Caddoans lived in grass lodges shaped somewhat like a huge beehive. The frameworks were made of poles planted in a circle and bent together at the top. The poles were covered thickly with grass or mats. Smoke came out through the space around the ends of the poles. Some Indians covered their houses with skins.

Hunting parties lived in tepees, made of poles and skins, which they took with them. With only dogs to drag the travois at first, the tepees had to be kept small, but when horses were acquired, the tepees became larger and larger, and the hunting trips longer and longer. At last, many of the Indians abandoned their farms and lived entirely in tepees, which could be taken along whenever they wanted to move. Many of these tepees were so large that it took many skins to cover them. These skins were usually decorated with pictures telling about the owners' feats in battle, for war was a glorious game with the Plains Indian.

The Indians got along well with the explorers and fur traders, because these men supplied them with precious knives and guns and blankets and did not drive them out of their homes. But the settlers took the Indians' lands and killed their game and pushed them ever westward. So the Indians struck back fiercely, again and again, until they were finally driven out or killed by the white man's diseases, against which the Indian had no defense. At one time, two white men infected the Mandans with smallpox and practically wiped them out, leaving less than two hundred of the original group that had numbered almost two thousand.

The Lewis and Clark Expedition

At the time that President Jefferson purchased the Louisiana Territory from France for the United States, the Indians were practically the only people living on the plains. The new territory was a vast, unknown region, and Jefferson sent out expeditions to explore it. Zebulon Pike, who later discovered Pike's Peak in Colorado, explored the upper Mississippi River. The most important expedition, however, was the one led by Jefferson's secretary, Meriwether Lewis, and William Clark.

Lewis and Clark were the first white men to cross the extent of what is now the United States. They kept detailed, day-by-day journals, in which they told about everything they saw, even the plants and animals.

In May, 1804, they began the trip at St. Louis, where their party had been assembling since the previous autumn. Their plan was to go up the Missouri River as far as they could and then go west from there. By November, they had reached the site of present-day Bismarck, North Dakota, where they made their camp for the winter. They called it Fort Mandan, in honor of the Mandan Indians, who were their only neighbors.

All the Indians they had met on their journey were friendly, and the Mandans were no exception. Living among them were a Shoshone woman named Sacajawea, and her husband, Toussaint Charbonneau, a French guide. Sacajawea's family lived on the Snake River in what is now Idaho, but she had been captured by raiding Indians. Charbonneau had bought her from her captors and made her his wife.

When the Lewis and Clark party left the Mandan Indians in the spring of 1805, Charbonneau and Sacajawea went with them as guides. Sacajawea had a tiny baby, which she usually carried strapped to her back. She was familiar with the wild, rugged country ahead of the expedition, and she was able to lead it through the best places to cross the Rocky Mountains. When she was re-united with her family on the Snake River, she persuaded her brother, who was a powerful chief, to aid the expedition.

After a stopover with her tribe, she and her husband continued with Lewis and Clark to the coast, where Sacajawea and the rest of the expedition had their first glimpse of the Pacific Ocean. They built Fort Clatsop, now Astoria, Oregon, as winter quarters.

On the return trip, the party separated after it had crossed the Rockies, part of the men going down the Yellowstone River and part of them down the Missouri River. The two parties came together again at the junction of the Yellowstone and Missouri.

Lewis and Clark returned to St. Louis in September, 1806, and the information they brought back with them concerning the land, the Indians, the animals and plants, and the climate of the country west of the Mississippi was to be extremely valuable in the settlement of the West. The expedition also helped to bolster the claim of the United States to the Oregon country.

Westward Ho!

In the years following the Lewis and Clark expedition, more and more effort turned to exploring and using the country west of the Missouri. For hundreds of miles, it was Indian territory. To the southwest was Santa Fe, thriving city of Spain and Mexico. On the Pacific Coast were American and Spanish settlements, reached by ships that sailed from Atlantic seaports around South America. In between, from the Missouri to the Pacific, there were no roads and very little communication of any kind.

The explorers went out, and the mountain men and the fur traders. They brought back tales of a fabulous country of prairies and mountains and rich river valleys. In the early 1820's, a few wagons went from the Missouri River to Santa Fe, and so the Santa Fe Trail began. In the 1830's, a few wagons went from the Missouri to Oregon, and started the Oregon Trail and, later, the California Trail.

The Santa Fe Trail crossed Kansas from the Missouri River, one branch going all the way to the Rocky Mountains and then heading southwest to Santa Fe, and the other crossing the Arkansas River, near where Dodge City now is, and going across the Cimarron to Santa Fe. The Oregon Trail headed northwest from the Missouri, the various branches meeting at the great valley of the Platte River. Here was a natural route into the Rocky Mountains, used for centuries by the Indians—a route that the wagons used on both the north and south banks of the Platte, all the way west through Nebraska. Scotts Bluff was the great landmark for turning northwest, and from there the trail went on through Wyoming's South Pass to divide in the mountains toward Oregon in the north and California in the south.

Over these trails, in the years that followed, thousands of people rode in big wagons with white canvas tops—the famous "prairie schooners"—moving all their possessions to the western frontier to set up new homes on the prairies or in the Oregon and California mountains and valleys. Settlers started west from one or another point on the Missouri—such places as St. Joseph and Independence and various points in Nebraska. They started in the spring of the year, and rode all summer to reach their destination. A wagon train was like a moving town. People lived in their wagons from day to day; marriages were performed along the way, babies were born, people died and were buried.

On the Santa Fe Trail, great freight wagons, pulled by oxen, carried goods of cotton and wool, silk and velvet, and the manufactured hardwares of the East, to trade in Santa Fe for furs and horses, and to sell for Spanish gold. The trains of wagons were called "bull trains," and the men who drove the oxen were "bullwhackers."

Trails to California Gold

When gold was discovered in California, in 1849, people had a new reason for heading west—to get rich quick. So the "Great Migration" was multiplied many times. People swarmed into the Missouri River towns, buying wagons there or bringing them from home, and made up tremendous trains to follow the Oregon and California trails. In the years of 1849 and 1850, nearly 100,000 people went west along the trails.

Stage coaches soon followed the trails, and people had a faster means of travel, if they could "travel light." The horses were urged along at top speed, and there were frequent relay stations where fresh horses could be exchanged for tired ones. The stage coaches carried mail, and so communication, too, was speeded up.

But not enough. People wanted a way to get letters back and forth as quickly as possible. So the pony express was established, and lonely riders sent their ponies headlong between relay stations, from Missouri to California. Even this was not fast enough. So, at last, the telegraph was built, following the routes of the overland trails.

Indian Troubles

In eastern Nebraska, the Pawnees and other tribes, while not warlike, took every opportunity to steal from the wagon trains. Farther west, the wagon trains were in danger of raids from the Kiowas and Comanches and others in Kansas, and the Sioux and Cheyenne in Nebraska. Stage coaches often had to have an escort of United States cavalrymen.

During the Civil War, when the United States Army was fighting in the East, the Indians rose against the western settlers. All through Kansas and Nebraska the Indians attacked the wagon trains and brought them to a halt. Stage coaches stopped running. Telegraph lines were torn down. Homes, stage stations, and even whole towns were burned. But the Civil War came to an end, and the cavalry came back to the West. Settlement could go on.

A Railroad to the Pacific

After the war, the Union Pacific Railroad was built through Nebraska, close along the Platte River and the Oregon Trail. With the Central Pacific building eastward from California, the two would meet in Utah to form one railroad from the Missouri to the Pacific Coast.

All through Nebraska, the railroad builders had to fight off Indians while they built; the construction workers had their rifles nearby, leaning against a stack of ties, and often had to stop laying ties to shoot Indians. Sometimes, after the track was laid and the trains were running, the Indians tore up the rails and wrecked the trains.

Along the way materials had to be brought from Omaha, but even before they could reach Omaha, the supplies had to come by boat across the river. There was no railroad bridge at Omaha until the whole railroad was finished. Then, as the track was finished, supplies were moved along to warehouses in whatever town was "end o' track." Kearney and North Platte and other towns served their turn as end o' track. Then the railroad moved on into Colorado, and into Wyoming and Utah. While the Union Pacific was building across Nebraska, its southern branch, the Kansas Pacific, was building across Kansas. So now, with railroads, the West was truly open for settlement.

Things to think about

What differences were there in the ways of life of the first people of the Plains and the later Indians of the region?

How did the coming of horses affect the Indians' way of life?

Why did white men first come to the Plains?

How did the Plains region become part of the United States?

Compare the different types of dwellings of the Plains Indians.

Why was the Lewis and Clark Expedition so important to the settling of this region?

How did developments in transportation speed up the settlement of the Plains States?

Life on the plains today

Natural Resources

The Plains States have a variety of natural resources, of which fertile soil, possessed in large amounts by every state, is the most important. The soil is richest in the areas which were once covered by glaciers or by ancient seas, and it is most valuable where the climate is humid enough to raise corn and other crops. But even in the semi-arid climates, the soil produces wild grasses which are harvested for hay or grazed by livestock.

Water, of course, is valuable, wherever it can be found. Some of the states have important underground reserves, which come to the surface through springs and artesian or driven wells. In most of the states, surface water, during flood periods, is stored in huge, man-made lakes, for irrigation purposes during dry periods. These reservoirs are often stocked with fish and serve as recreation areas for thousands of people.

Coal, petroleum and natural gas, limestone, and clay for making bricks are found in most of the states in varying amounts. Some of the minerals and stones found in a few of the states are lead, zinc, gypsum, granite, marble, gold, silver, and uranium.

Trees are scarce in the Plains States except along streams and in places where they have been planted since the area was settled. Missouri's mountain areas are heavily wooded, and so are the Black Hills in South Dakota and the Turtle and Pembina mountains in North Dakota.

Farm and Rangelands

Agriculture plays a very important part in the economic life of the Plains States. Here in the western section of the Corn Belt, Iowa, northern Missouri, and eastern Nebraska produce some of the finest corn in the United States. Kansas and the Dakotas are noted for their wheat.

Settlers shunned the plains area in the early days because they did not think it would make good farming land. Most of it was open range land, where great herds of buffalo fed. After the Civil War, during the colorful days of the Old West, large herds of cattle were driven from Texas to the open range lands for summer grazing, before they were shipped east. Huge cattle ranches sprang up, with thousands of acres in each ranch.

Land became scarce as more and more people pressed westward. The settlers discovered that the soil of the plains was deep and rich, and they fenced much of the land, drained it and planted it to crops. Bitterness arose between the settlers and the cattlemen because herds could no longer be moved across the plains and there was little grazing land left for the cattle. When power machinery was invented that could plow many acres a day or harvest many acres of grain, the farmers planted vast areas to wheat and other grain crops. They even tried to farm the dry western areas.

Then a dreadful thing happened. Droughts came and dried up the plowed land into fine dust, which was picked up by high winds and whirled away. For many days and nights, the dust storms were so bad that a person could hardly see his hand before his face. Crops were spoiled, and good topsoil was blown away. The farmers were ruined, and many of them had to move away.

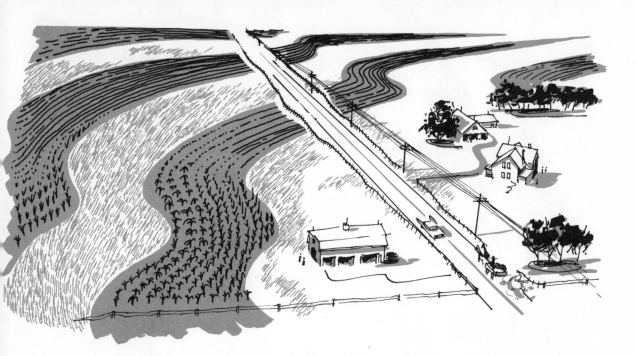

When rain fell again and the dust settled, the farmers who were left learned better ways to farm. Contour plowing is often used now if the land slopes even a little. Each furrow is plowed around the slope, so that water, instead of running down the slope, is caught in the furrows and held in the ground. This method also keeps the soil from blowing away, or washing with the water. Strip cropping is often used with contour farming, with strips of close-growing, moisture-holding crops, such as alfalfa or clover, alternating with strips of small grain, corn, and other crops. A heavy cover of grass is kept on the driest land, and this land is used for livestock grazing.

Winter wheat, introduced into Kansas by Mennonite settlers from Russia, has made that state the leading hard-wheat state in the nation. Winter wheat is planted in the fall and has a good start by spring, so that it is ready for early harvest. Spring wheat, which is grown largely in the Dakotas, is planted in the spring and harvested in the fall..

Oats, rye, barley, soybeans, and alfalfa are also important crops in the Plains States, and sugar beets and potatoes are grown in some sections. A large part of the grain and fodder crops are fed to cattle, sheep, hogs, and poultry, much of it right on the farm where the crops are grown. Many of the beef cattle are brought in from the West, to be fattened on corn before they are shipped to city stockyards.

Gold in the Black Hills

Although the Plains States are noted more for agriculture than for mining, they do have some valuable minerals. In fact, the discovery of gold in the Black Hills in 1874, by General George Armstrong Custer's expedition, led to one of the most colorful gold rushes in our country's history. It also led to one of the worst Indian wars, in which Custer and his whole command were wiped out.

The Black Hills were the Sioux' sacred "Paha Sapa," which Custer's expedition invaded, although the land had been given to the Indians "forever" under treaty with the United States. When news of the gold discovery leaked out, prospectors stampeded into the sacred hills in buggies, wagons, and stagecoaches, on foot and horseback. Nothing could stop them. The "Homestake" mine near Deadwood turned out to be the richest claim, and is still one of the world's leading gold mines.

The discovery and development of the great oil and natural gas fields in the Plains States were almost as dramatic as the discovery of gold, and saved many a farmer in the drought areas from ruin. Valuable beds of coal are also found in every state, and limestone is in most of them. Lead is mined in large quantities in Missouri and to a lesser extent in some of the other states. An interesting mineral found in almost every state is clay, used for making bricks and tile. Some kinds are used for making dishes.

Manufacturing and Processing

Manufacturing was going on in the Plains region for quite a while before the settlers moved in—some thousands of years, in fact! Spear points and other weapons and tools of flint and stone, believed to have been made between ten and twenty thousand years ago, have been discovered. Beautifully designed pottery, shell beads, and other artifacts of a later date have also been found.

The first manufacturing done for the settlers was probably plowshares hammered out by the local blacksmith and, perhaps, iron pots and kettles made in his spare time.

The leading processing industries are based on the region's own agricultural products. Flour milling in Kansas, an important industry in the Plains States, was started by a Wyandot Indian and was horse powered. Water power was used later, and after that, steam.

Meat packing, one of the region's greatest industries, began when herds of cattle were driven from Texas to railroad shipping points over the Chisholm Trail and other trails. The invention of refrigerated railroad cars enabled the meat to be processed at the shipping point and sent direct to eastern markets. Other processed foods include canned and frozen fruits and vegetables, candy, sugar, animal and vegetable fats and oils, cereals, dairy products—butter, cheese, and ice cream—and feeds for livestock and poultry.

Leading industries include the refining of petroleum and the manufacturing of transportation equipment and agricultural machinery, airplane parts, fertilizers, and stone, clay, and glass products. Other products range all the way from house trailers and mobile homes to fountain pens and fresh-water-pearl buttons. Publishing and printing are important and interesting industries in the Plains States.

Transportation

Transportation began across the Plains region with the great overland trails—the Santa Fe, the Oregon, and California trails—over which the wagon trains moved ever westward. Often these wagon trains were a mile in length. Freighting companies were organized and hauled thousands of tons of freight in huge wagons drawn by six-, eight- or twelve-mule and ox teams. Now U.S. 30, known as the Lincoln Highway, and the Union Pacific Railroad roughly follow the route of the old Oregon Trail.

Indians, explorers, and fur traders traveled on the rivers. They went down the Mississippi to its junction with the Missouri, then up the Missouri and its tributaries. Keelboats and, later, steamboats followed the Missouri into the Dakotas. Settlers came down the Ohio or the Mississippi and went up the Missouri to St. Joseph or Independence or Westport Landing—later, Kansas City—where they outfitted prairie schooners and joined the wagon trains westward. Eventually, some of them settled in the Plains States.

A fine system of highways and railroads now crosses the plains, and jet planes roar overhead. Thousands of trucks, carrying freight from all over the nation, travel the highways every day. Kansas City, St. Louis, and Omaha are noted as transportation centers.

The People of the Plains

The first people who had permanent homes in the Plains region, of whom we have any record, were the Mound Builders in the extreme eastern section of the region. In the Missouri River Valley were the later Indian farmers whose village sites have been excavated along streams. Today, the whole Indian population is less than 45,000, and these are mainly on reservations in the Dakotas, with several thousand in Nebraska, and a few hundred in Iowa.

In the 1830's, after the Louisiana Territory had been explored and opened for settlement, pioneers poured across the Mississippi River into Iowa and Missouri. The first settlers in Iowa were mainly from New England, while those in Missouri came from the southern states. They brought their Negro slaves with them, and set up cotton and tobacco plantations. Other settlers came from the mountains of Tennessee and Kentucky and settled in the Ozarks, bringing their customs and folklore with them. Many of these mountain people still live the same way today as did their ancestors who settled in the southern mountains in the early days of our country. Their folkways and traditions, handed down through generations, are an interesting and colorful part of America's culture.

White people, except fur trappers and traders, were slow to come into the western plains. There were just too many unfriendly Indians!

After the railroads were built and the Indians subdued, many settlers began coming to the western plains. Towns sprang up along the railroads and became shipping points for agricultural products. The famous cattle drives started between Texas and such Kansas "cow towns" as Abilene and Dodge City, providing background for Old West personalities like Wyatt Earp and Wild Bill Hickok.

Many Europeans—Germans, Russians, Scandinavians, Dutch, Czechs, Irish, and others—seeking religious and political freedom and a happier way of life, were attracted to the Plains States. In 1855 a German religious sect founded a settlement at Amana, Iowa, which remained communal until 1932. Russian Mennonites, in 1874, introduced their Red Turkey hard winter wheat into Kansas. The Bohemians, or Czechs, founded the little town of Spillville, where Antonin Dvorak received inspiration for the New World Symphony.

The Plains States have given three presidents to the United States: Herbert Hoover, who was born at West Branch, Iowa, Harry Truman, from Independence, Missouri, and Dwight D. Eisenhower, from Abilene, Kansas. Other noted people who were either born in the Plains States or lived there include General John J. Pershing, General Omar N. Bradley, James J. Hill, George Washington Carver, John L. Lewis, Billy Sunday, and Thomas Hart Benton, the statesman, and his grandnephew, Thomas Hart Benton, the painter.

The Arts and Artists of the Plains

The arts and folklore of many different peoples have blended to form the rich and varied culture of the Plains States. A part of the Plains tradition is the graceful and colorful art of the Plains Indians, expressed first in the stories painted on their tepees and buffalo hides, in the porcupine-quill and bear-claw embroidery and beadwork that decorated their clothing, and even in their warbonnets and war paint.

From the South came beautiful music, lovely dances, and gracious living. The folkways and customs of the mountain people, and the ballads of the cowboys became a part of Plains culture. Important, too, are the varied traditions of the European immigrants who brought to the plains their own folk songs and folk dances, their ideas about architecture, and their love for the great masters in art and music.

These states, lying between the Great Lakes and the Rocky Mountains, have given many great writers, musicians, actors, and painters to the nation. Samuel Clemens—Mark Twain to us—brought us the magic of river-boat life on the Mississippi. The background for his books about two boys, *Tom Sawyer* and *Huckleberry Finn*, is similar to his own boyhood background in the Mississippi port town of Hannibal, Missouri.

Hamlin Garland wrote about the Plains States in several of his books, including *A Son of the Middle Border* and *A Daughter of the Middle Border*. The novel *Shepherd of the Hills*, by Harold Bell Wright, was laid in the Ozarks. Iowa authors include Ruth Suckow, Phil Stong, James Norman Hall, and MacKinlay Kantor. The poets Sara Teasdale and Eugene Field were born in Missouri, and Edgar Lee Masters was born in Kansas.

A great journalist of Kansas, William Allen White, made his newspaper, the Emporia *Gazette,* famous all over the country. He wrote a number of novels, essays, and books on public affairs, and his editorial, "Mary White," written on the accidental death of his only daughter, has become a classic.

50

The artists of the plains painted the common man as they saw him, in his ordinary walks of life. George Catlin came to the plains as early as 1832 and devoted his life to painting the Indians. Thomas Hart Benton's pictures, though realistic, show the modern influence. His "Custer's Last Stand," painted with sure, vigorous strokes, is one of his most popular. His murals in the Missouri State House at Jefferson City aroused a great controversy at the time they were painted, but now the citizens of the state point to them with great pride.

John Steuart Curry's murals in the Kansas State House at Topeka have become famous throughout the nation, especially the dominant center figure of John Brown. Grant Wood, who painted Iowa rural life as he saw it, was another controversial figure. His "Daughters of the Revolution" and "American Gothic" brought bitter protests from some people and enthusiastic approval from others.

Architecture in the Plains States ranges all the way from handsome southern homes in Missouri to sod houses on the plains of Nebraska and Kansas. The tall, graceful capitols of Nebraska and North Dakota are fine examples of modern architecture. The Wainwright Building in St. Louis, considered by many to be the nation's first real skyscraper, was designed by Louis Sullivan, the teacher of Frank Lloyd Wright. Wright himself designed a home and a hotel which now stand in Mason City, Iowa.

Things to think about

Why is soil the most important natural resource in the Plains States?

How do manufacturing and industry depend on the resources of the land?

What events caused rapid increases in the population of the Plains region?

In what ways are the arts of the region characteristic of the Plains?

Enchantment of the plains

The sweeping prairies and great, man-made lakes, the magic of the Ozarks and Black Hills, the fantastic badlands, the rivers and springs and fairyland caverns, the vivid spring green of the cornfields as they march in endless, diminishing squares toward the horizon — these are some of the things that make the Plains region a true land of enchantment.

There are so many wonderful places to see that it would take months to visit them all — the huge Lake of the Ozarks in Missouri, "Little Switzerland" in Iowa, the Old West "cow towns" and long strings of white-faced cattle winding over the prairie in Kansas, the state parks in Nebraska, the Black Hills and Badlands in South Dakota, the Garrison Reservoir and the Theodore Roosevelt National Memorial Park in North Dakota.

Everywhere we go in the Plains States we find reminders of the early history of the country — in fact, even of prehistory, for ancient Indian mounds are plentiful in the·eastern section. Some of the most outstanding are Iowa's Effigy Mounds near McGregor, which are in the forms of birds and other animals. They are preserved in a national monument. Near Salina, Kansas, is a burial pit containing the remains of more than one hundred prehistoric Indians. A building has been erected over the pit to preserve the skeletons, as well as to house a large collection of Indian artifacts.

Many communities bring back the Old West in plays, pageantry, and rodeos. The Indians re-live their past in old and colorful dances and ceremonials. Early-day forts, homes, and even villages are preserved just as they were when they were occupied many years ago.

Early-Day Forts

A few miles south of Mandan, North Dakota, the blockhouse of Fort Abraham Lincoln still stands from which General George A. Custer and his men rode off to their deaths in the fatal Battle of the Little Big Horn, in southeastern Montana. From the top of the blockhouse one can get a sweeping view of the surrounding country. Nearby are Indian earth lodges reconstructed to look just as they did when the Indians lived in them. The outdoor drama, "Trail West!" given every summer in the George Armstrong Custer Memorial Amphitheatre, tells the story of Custer and his last ride.

Another historic old fort in North Dakota is Fort Totten, on the Fort Totten Indian Reservation, just south of Devil's Lake. This fort was built in 1867 as a protection for people who were making the long trip from Minnesota to Montana. The buildings, grouped around a hollow square, are in a good state of preservation.

Nebraska's Fort Kearny State Park preserves the original parade ground and some of the buildings of Old Fort Kearny. And Kansas has two historic forts still in use — Fort Leavenworth, dating from 1827, and Fort Riley, established in 1852. Fort Riley, on the Santa Fe Trail, is one of the largest military reserves in the nation.

Towns with a Past

Many historic towns in the Plains States give us fascinating glimpses of the past at the same time that they speak of the present. Abilene, Kansas, famous Old West cow town, has now become even more famous as the boyhood home of former President Dwight Eisenhower. Near Dodge City, another famous Kansas cow town, the deep ruts of the Santa Fe Trail can still be seen. Council Grove, on the Santa Fe Trail, for many years was the last outfitting post between the Missouri River and Santa Fe. There are many historic buildings here, and two oak trees of special interest. One is the Post Office Oak, where letters were left for passing caravans; the other is the stump of Council Oak, where the right of way for the Santa Fe Trail was obtained by treaty with the Indians in 1825.

Deadwood, South Dakota, one of the liveliest "ghost" towns of the West, brings back the rip-roaring Wild West of early days with its historic buildings, old mines, and Mount Moriah Cemetery, where Wild Bill Hickok and Calamity Jane are buried.

Ste. Genevieve, Missouri, settled by the French in 1732, is quite a different historic town, with its old French homes and cemetery. Bolduc House is now a museum, open to the public.

Pony Express Stations

Remains of some of the stations still stand along the pony express route. The express stables have been preserved at St. Joseph, Missouri, starting point of the route, and the original Hollenberg Station, near Hanover, Kansas, now houses a museum. The remains of another station may still be seen at Gothenburg, Nebraska.

Memorials

The tall, graceful Floyd Monument, on a bluff overlooking the Missouri River near Sioux City, Iowa, commemorates the Lewis and Clark Expedition and marks the burial place of one of their men, Sergeant Charles Floyd, who died on the trip. Another national shrine is the birthplace of former President Herbert Hoover, at West Branch, Iowa.

National Parks and Monuments

Here and there throughout the country, Congress and the President have set aside tracts of land containing unusual scenic or historical values. These are to be preserved, with as little change as possible, for the benefit of all the people in the nation and for their posterity. They are under the direction of the National Park Service, and most of them are called either national parks or national monuments.

Many of the national parks and monuments in the Plains States, such as Iowa's Effigy Mounds National Monument, are memorials to the past. The George Washington Carver National Monument, in Missouri, contains the birthplace and childhood home of this famous Negro scientist.

In Nebraska the Homestead National Monument preserves the first claim filed under the Homestead Act of 1862. Chimney Rock National Historic Site contains a tall rock shaft that guided covered wagons crossing Nebraska on the Oregon Trail. The deep tracks of the Oregon Trail can still be seen crossing through the Scotts Bluff National Monument, which preserves a high bluff that also served as a landmark on the trail. The trail goes through Mitchell Pass, and we can walk along it for a mile on the west slope of the bluff. A museum at monument headquarters contains rocks and fossils, Indian and pioneer relics, dioramas, watercolors, and the paintings of William H. Jackson, famous pioneer artist.

Theodore Roosevelt National Memorial Park

The Theodore Roosevelt National Memorial Park, in North Dakota, commemorates former President Theodore Roosevelt, who made important contributions to the conservation of the nation's natural resources. The park is in three units along the Little Missouri River. It totals about 110 square miles and preserves part of Roosevelt's Elkhorn Ranch site, as well as a large area of badlands, which have been eroded by wind and water into strange, colorful shapes. A herd of buffaloes inhabits the park, as well as pronghorn antelope and several towns of black-tailed prairie dogs, which are not dogs at all, but belong to the squirrel family. An outdoor drama, "Old Four-Eyes," which depicts the adventures of Roosevelt in North Dakota, is given during the summer months at Medora, near the South Unit of the park.

Black Hills and Badlands

In South Dakota are several interesting national monuments and a national park. Badlands National Monument is filled with fantastically beautiful rock and soil formations that change in color as the light changes. Many fossils of bygone animals have been found here, some of which are on display at the South Dakota School of Mines at Rapid City. Many present-day animals live here, too — coyotes, porcupines, raccoons, cottontails and jack rabbits, prairie dogs and other ground squirrels. The hundreds of little chipmunks that scamper about have taken on the pale color of their surroundings.

In the Black Hills, Mount Rushmore National Memorial contains the awe-inspiring giant sculptured heads of four of our presidents — Washington, Jefferson, Lincoln, and Theodore Roosevelt. They were carved by Gutzon Borglum, noted sculptor, and finished, after his death, by his son, Lincoln Borglum. School children from all over the nation collected pennies to help pay for the Memorial.

In Jewel Cave National Monument, the walls and ceilings of some of the rooms are lined with beautiful crystals, ranging in color from a light brown to a dark shade of chocolate. The colors in other rooms shade from light green to dark green and bronze. This cave is kept as primitive as possible and is not lighted. Visitors going through it carry gasoline lanterns.

Another, very different, cave is found in the Wind Cave National Park. This fairyland is electrically lighted, and on its walls and ceilings are many beautiful formations and crystal-lined cavities. The cave is noted for the rare boxwork formation on the ceiling of the Elks Room. Wind Cave Park is equally popular for its surface area of prairie and forest, where many kinds of animals roam — buffalo, elk, deer, antelopes, coyotes — in fact, most of the animals seen by travelers to the early West. Several prairie-dog towns are a feature here, too. The buffalo herds in this park and the adjoining Custer State Park are among the largest in the United States, and they are a sight well worth seeing.

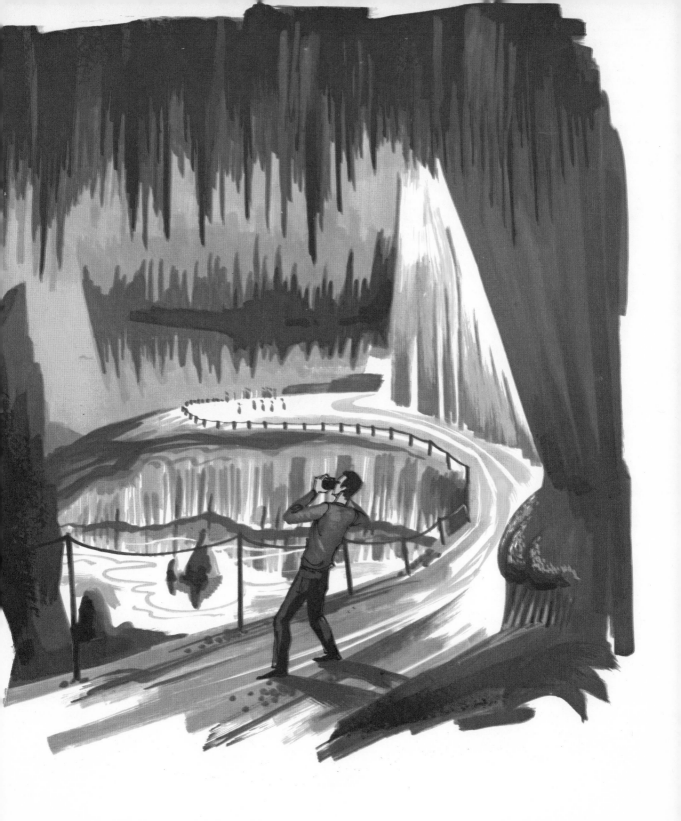

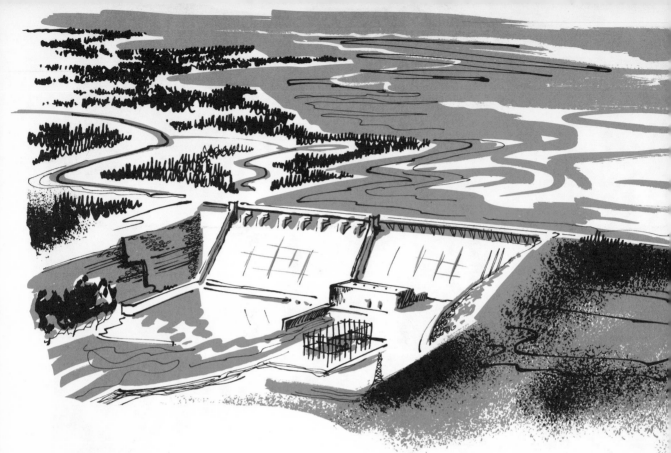

Man-Made Lakes

There's hardly a state in the Plains region that doesn't have at least one huge, man-made lake. Missouri's Lake of the Ozarks, with its twisting, wooded shoreline more than 1,300 miles long, has dozens of resorts and state parks. Lake Taneycomo and Table Rock Reservoir, and Bull Shoals and Norfork lakes, which Missouri shares with Arkansas, are equally popular resort areas.

Garrison Reservoir, stretching for 150 miles along the Missouri River in North Dakota, and South Dakota's Oahe and Fort Randall reservoirs and Lewis and Clark Lake, on the Nebraska line, make up the "Great Lakes of the Missouri." Besides being splendid recreation areas, they help to keep the mighty Missouri from washing away homes and farms during the flood season.

Nebraska has Lake McConaughy and shares the Lewis and Clark Lake with South Dakota. Kansas, with few natural lakes, has Kirwin and Kanopolis reservoirs and numerous smaller man-made lakes.

Things to think about

How have important events and places from the history of this region
been preserved?

What special monuments in the Plains States commemorate men who
have been famous in our country's history?

What are some of the natural wonders to be found in the Panoramic
Plains?

Describe the wildlife of the Plains and their habitats.

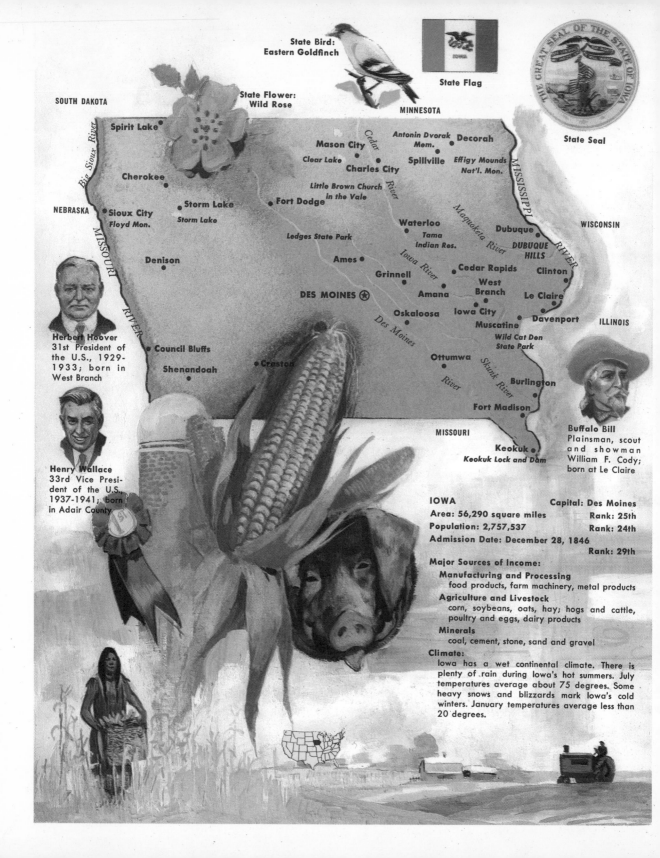

State Bird:
Eastern Goldfinch

State Flag

THE GREAT SEAL OF THE STATE OF IOWA

State Seal

State Flower:
Wild Rose

SOUTH DAKOTA

MINNESOTA

Spirit Lake

Big Sioux River

Mason City
Clear Lake
Charles City

Cedar River

Antonin Dvorak Mem.
Decorah
Spillville
Effigy Mounds Nat'l. Mon.

MISSISSIPPI RIVER

WISCONSIN

Cherokee

Little Brown Church in the Vale

NEBRASKA

Sioux City
Floyd Mon.

Storm Lake
Storm Lake

Fort Dodge

Waterloo
Tama Indian Res.

Maquoketa River

Dubuque
DUBUQUE HILLS

MISSOURI RIVER

Denison

Ledges State Park

Ames

Grinnell

Iowa River

Cedar Rapids
West Branch

Clinton
Le Claire

Herbert Hoover
31st President of
the U.S., 1929-
1933; born in
West Branch

DES MOINES ✪

Amana

Oskaloosa

Iowa City
Muscatine
Wild Cat Den State Park

Davenport

ILLINOIS

Des Moines

Council Bluffs

Shenandoah

Creston

Ottumwa

Skunk River

Burlington

Henry Wallace
33rd Vice Presi-
dent of the U.S.,
1937-1941; born
in Adair County

River

Fort Madison

MISSOURI

Keokuk
Keokuk Lock and Dam

Buffalo Bill
Plainsman, scout
and showman
William F. Cody;
born at Le Claire

IOWA
Area: 56,290 square miles
Population: 2,757,537
Admission Date: December 28, 1846

Capital: Des Moines
Rank: 25th
Rank: 24th

Rank: 29th

Major Sources of Income:
    Manufacturing and Processing
        food products, farm machinery, metal products
    Agriculture and Livestock
        corn, soybeans, oats, hay; hogs and cattle,
        poultry and eggs, dairy products
    Minerals
        coal, cement, stone, sand and gravel
Climate:
    Iowa has a wet continental climate. There is
    plenty of rain during Iowa's hot summers. July
    temperatures average about 75 degrees. Some
    heavy snows and blizzards mark Iowa's cold
    winters. January temperatures average less than
    20 degrees.

Iowa

Iowa, the richest farming state in the Union, lies between two great rivers, the Mississippi on her east and the Missouri on her west. Ice sheets covered most of the state at least four times, leaving the land flat or gently rolling, and with deep, fertile soil. The climate, too, is ideal for fine crops, with its heavy winter snows, wet springs, and long, hot, humid summers. Corn is the leading crop, followed by soybeans and oats. Most of the corn is fed to Iowa's livestock, and to the hogs and beef cattle brought in from the western plains to be fattened.

Important Whens and Whats in the Making of Iowa

1673 Marquette and Jolliet discover the Upper Missouri and the land that is now Iowa.

1788 Julien Dubuque obtains a grant from the Spanish to mine lead at the present site of Dubuque.

1799 The first apple orchard is planted.

1803 The Iowa region, part of the territory ceded by Spain to France, is sold to the United States in the Louisiana Purchase.

1804 Lewis and Clark pass through Iowa country.

1820 Iowa settlement starts in Lee County.

1832 Black Hawk War breaks the strength of the Sauk and the Fox Indians.

1838 The Iowa region becomes a separate Territory.

1846 Iowa is admitted to the Union as the 29th state.

Iowa's level surface is well suited to scientific mechanized farming, and the tractor was invented in this state. Hybrid corn was developed in Iowa, and the State Experiment Station works constantly to improve the quality of farm products and to find new uses for them.

In recent years, Iowa's industrial income has been larger than her income from agriculture, but much of her manufacturing and processing — such as the dressing of poultry, canning of vegetables, and dairy products — is based on her agricultural products.

Barges on the Mississippi and the Missouri rivers transport raw materials and finished products. The nation's largest roller-gate dam, on the Mississippi at Davenport, operates even when the river is frozen.

Iowa's rich farms and handsome homes are a sight worth seeing, but the state has many scenic attractions as well, many of which are protected in state parks. Wild Cat Den State Park, for instance, preserves an ancient gristmill and unusual rock formations; Maquoketa Caves State Park contains limestone caves, a natural bridge, and an enormous balanced rock.

Only one ice sheet covered the northeastern corner of the state, leaving a lovely scenic area known as "Little Switzerland." To the east are McGregor and McGregor Heights, on a great bluff above the Mississippi River. Pike's Peak State Park and Effigy Mounds National Monument are nearby.

Farther west, at Festina, is the unique little St. Anthony of Padua Chapel, known as the "smallest cathedral in the world." This chapel, which seats only eight persons, is twelve feet by sixteen feet in size and has a complete miniature altar. It was built by a soldier in Napoleon's army who came to Iowa in 1846. Southwest of Festina, at Nashua, is the ninety-year-old "Little Brown Church in the Vale," visited by thousands of tourists every year.

In northwest Iowa is an area known as the "lake region," where there are numerous lakes, complete with fishing, boating, and swimming. Some of the larger ones are Spirit Lake, East and West Okoboji lakes, near the Minnesota line, and Storm Lake, to the south.

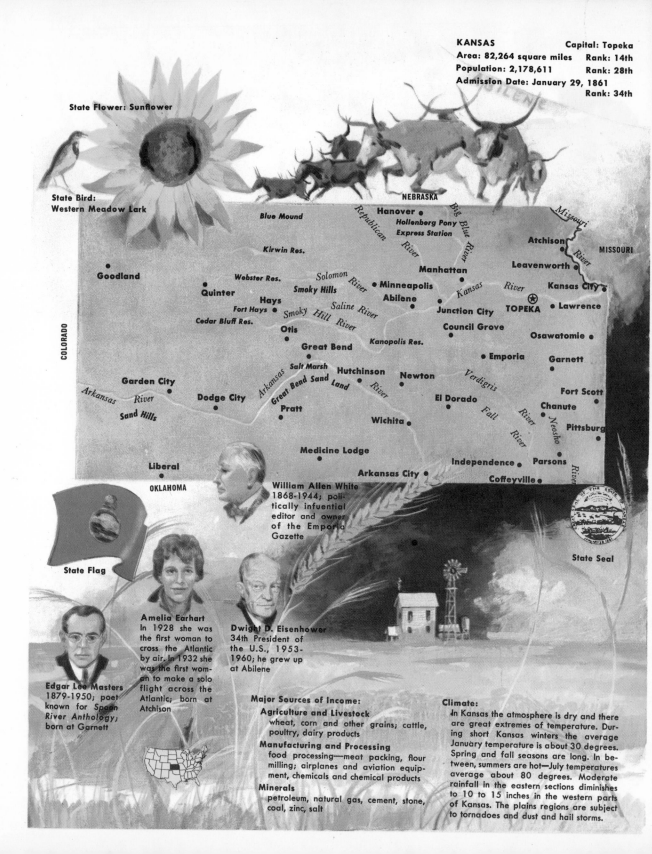

KANSAS   Capital: Topeka
Area: 82,264 square miles   Rank: 14th
Population: 2,178,611   Rank: 28th
Admission Date: January 29, 1861
Rank: 34th

State Flower: Sunflower

State Bird:
Western Meadow Lark

NEBRASKA

MISSOURI

COLORADO

OKLAHOMA

Blue Mound
Hanover
Hollenberg Pony
Express Station
Kirwin Res.
Atchison
Leavenworth
MISSOURI
Goodland
Webster Res.
Smoky Hills
Manhattan
Kansas City
Quinter
Minneapolis
Hays
Abilene
Junction City
TOPEKA
Lawrence
Fort Hays
Saline River
Cedar Bluff Res.
Smoky Hill River
Council Grove
Otis
Kanopolis Res.
Osawatomie
Great Bend
Emporia
Garnett
Salt Marsh
Hutchinson
Garden City
Great Bend Sand Land
Newton
Verdigris
Dodge City
River
Fort Scott
Pratt
El Dorado
Chanute
Sand Hills
Wichita
Pittsburg
Medicine Lodge
Liberal
Independence
Parsons
Arkansas City
Coffeyville

Republican River
Big Blue River
Missouri River
Solomon River
Kansas River
Arkansas River
Neosho River
Fall River

William Allen White
1868-1944; politically infuential
editor and owner
of the Emporia
Gazette

State Seal

State Flag

Amelia Earhart
In 1928 she was
the first woman to
cross the Atlantic
by air. In 1932 she
was the first woman to make a solo
flight across the
Atlantic; born at
Atchison

Dwight D. Eisenhower
34th President of
the U.S., 1953-
1960; he grew up
at Abilene

Edgar Lee Masters
1879-1950; poet
known for *Spoon
River Anthology*;
born at Garnett

Major Sources of Income:

Agriculture and Livestock
wheat, corn and other grains; cattle,
poultry, dairy products

Manufacturing and Processing
food processing—meat packing, flour
milling; airplanes and aviation equipment, chemicals and chemical products

Minerals
petroleum, natural gas, cement, stone,
coal, zinc, salt

Climate:
In Kansas the atmosphere is dry and there
are great extremes of temperature. During short Kansas winters the average
January temperature is about 30 degrees.
Spring and fall seasons are long. In between, summers are hot—July temperatures
average about 80 degrees. Moderate
rainfall in the eastern sections diminishes
to 10 to 15 inches in the western parts
of Kansas. The plains regions are subject
to tornadoes and dust and hail storms.

Once described by explorers as "unfit for cultivation," Kansas is now characterized by sleek, well-fed Hereford cattle and golden fields of wheat. Kansas lies in the center of the forty-eight states, exclusive of Hawaii and Alaska. A cairn, near Lebanon, marks the exact geographical center; surrounding it is a landscaped area with picnic grounds and shelter house.

Kansas slopes gradually from an elevation of more than 4,000 feet on the Colorado line to about 700 feet on the eastern border. The treeless High Plains in the west are gently rolling, but their slope, as they meet the prairies in the east, is marked by eroded badlands, buttes, and chalk pinnacles, such as Monument Rocks, north of Scott City. Another example is Castle Rock, in Gove County, near Quinter. In the east are small rounded hills and low cliffs and canyons. The state has few natural lakes, but many man-made ones have been built.

Important Whens and Whats in the Making of Kansas

1541 Coronado leads Spanish troops into the Kansas region in a futile search for gold.

1682 Through La Salle, France claims all the territory drained by the Mississippi, including the Kansas region.

1763 Spain receives the land of Kansas, along with other territory, from France.

1800 The Kansas region goes back to the French.

1803 The United States obtains the land through the Louisiana Purchase.

1806 Zebulon Pike explores Kansas.

1827 Fort Leavenworth, the region's first permanent settlement, is founded.

1854 Kansas becomes a Territory.

1861 Kansas is admitted to the Union as the 34th state.

The great wheat fields of the western plains helped to make Kansas the nation's leading wheat-producing state. Colby, situated in the heart of the western wheat lands, is the self-styled "Golden Buckle on the Wheat Belt."

In extremely dry weather, heavy dust storms occur in western Kansas.

Kansas stands high among the states in the production of gasoline and natural gas, and salt is another important mineral product. There are large salt mines near Hutchinson and Lyons, with salt-processing plants at both places.

The history of Kansas was turbulent from the start. When the Kansas-Nebraska Bill was passed in 1854, creating the Territory of Kansas and leaving it up to the people in the Territory whether slavery would be allowed, a fight began immediately to keep Kansas a free state. Anti-slavery people rushed in from the North and pro-slavery people came in from Missouri. For several years "bleeding Kansas" was a battlefield for these two factions.

John Brown's Pottawatomie Massacre, in which his forces killed five pro-slavery men, was a part of this war. The free-state people finally won the struggle, and Kansas entered the Union as a free state just before the start of the Civil War. The John Brown Battleground Memorial Park preserves John Brown's cabin at Osawatomie.

The coming of the railroads after the war brought the cattle drives and the colorful cow towns, from which the cattle were shipped east. Then settlement of the western plains and fencing of the land brought violent conflict between the cattlemen and the settlers. Later, "dust-bowl" conditions were created by overgrazing and unwise plowing of land too dry for cultivation.

Today, Kansas has solved many of her problems, and her people can be justly proud of their "Sunflower State."

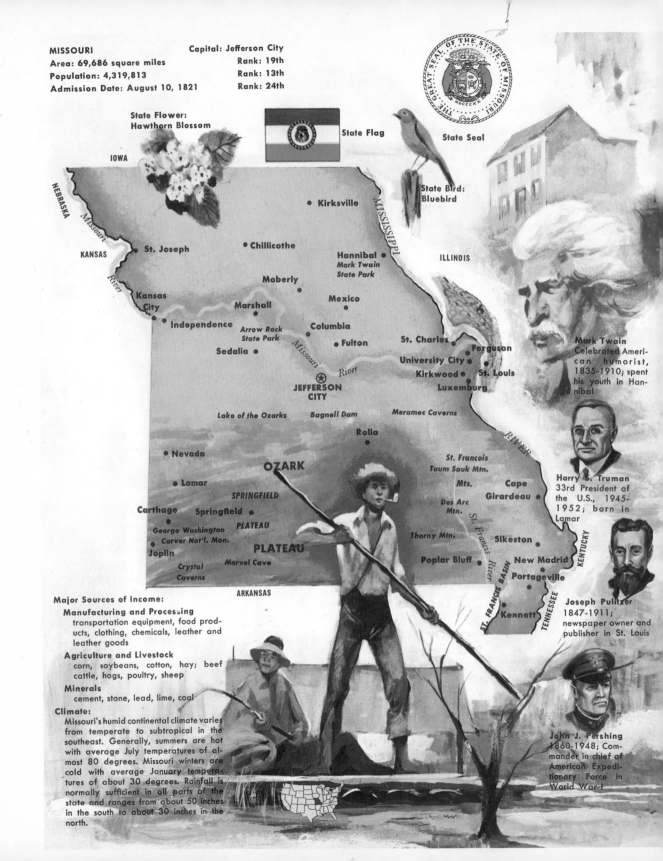

MISSOURI

Area: 69,686 square miles
Population: 4,319,813
Admission Date: August 10, 1821

Capital: Jefferson City
Rank: 19th
Rank: 13th
Rank: 24th

THE GREAT SEAL OF THE STATE OF MISSOURI · MDCCCXX

State Flower:
Hawthorn Blossom

State Flag

State Seal

State Bird:
Bluebird

IOWA

NEBRASKA

KANSAS

Missouri River

• Kirksville

MISSISSIPPI

• St. Joseph

• Chillicothe

Hannibal
Mark Twain
State Park

ILLINOIS

• Moberly

Kansas
City

• Marshall

Mexico

Independence

Arrow Rock
State Park

Columbia

St. Charles

• Sedalia

Missouri River

• Fulton

University City

Ferguson

Kirkwood

St. Louis

JEFFERSON
CITY

Luxemburg

Lake of the Ozarks

Bagnell Dam

Meramec Caverns

Rolla

RIVER

• Nevada

St. Francois
Taum Sauk Mtn.

OZARK

Mts.

Cape
Girardeau

• Lamar

SPRINGFIELD

Des Arc
Mtn.

Carthage

Springfield •

PLATEAU

St. Francis River

George Washington
Carver Nat'l. Mon.

PLATEAU

Thorny Mtn.

Sikeston

Joplin

Marvel Cave

Poplar Bluff

New Madrid

KENTUCKY

Crystal
Caverns

Portageville

ARKANSAS

ST. FRANCIS BASIN

Kennett

TENNESSEE

Mark Twain
Celebrated American humorist,
1835-1910; spent
his youth in Hannibal

Harry S. Truman
33rd President of
the U.S., 1945-
1952; born in
Lamar

Joseph Pulitzer
1847-1911;
newspaper owner and
publisher in St. Louis

John J. Pershing
1860-1948; Commander in chief of
American Expeditionary Force in
World War I

Major Sources of Income:

Manufacturing and Processing
transportation equipment, food products, clothing, chemicals, leather and
leather goods

Agriculture and Livestock
corn, soybeans, cotton, hay; beef
cattle, hogs, poultry, sheep

Minerals
cement, stone, lead, lime, coal

Climate:

Missouri's humid continental climate varies
from temperate to subtropical in the
southeast. Generally, summers are hot
with average July temperatures of almost 80 degrees. Missouri winters are
cold with average January temperatures of about 30 degrees. Rainfall is
normally sufficient in all parts of the
state and ranges from about 50 inches
in the south to about 30 inches in the
north.

The state of Missouri has practically everything — prairies and mountains; big cities, quiet rural countrysides with lovely old southern homes; caves that are underground fairylands; great man-made lakes and enormous springs and rivers where you can take float trips and fish as you float.

Missouri is bordered by eight states; only one other state, Tennessee, borders on that many. Illinois and Kentucky are on the east, with Tennessee at the southeast corner, which is known as the "Bootheel," or Delta. Arkansas is on the south of Missouri, Oklahoma at the southwest corner, Kansas on the west, Nebraska at the northwest corner, and Iowa on the north.

Important Whens and Whats in the Making of Missouri

1541 De Soto is a visitor to the region.

1715 The French discover lead at Mine La Motte.

1735 Ste. Genevieve, founded by the French, is the first permanent settlement of the region.

1764 St. Louis is founded by the French.

1803 The United States obtains the Missouri region from France as part of the Louisiana Purchase.

1804 Lewis and Clark start out from St. Louis on their westward journey.

1812 Missouri is organized as a separate Territory.

1820 The Missouri Compromise bill is passed, allowing Missouri to enter the Union as a slave state.

1821 Missouri is admitted to the Union as the 24th state.

1836 Missouri's present boundaries are established.

The Mississippi River flows along Missouri's eastern border, and the Missouri River cuts across the state, separating the glaciated area from the unglaciated. South of the Missouri River are the scenic Ozark Mountains and huge man-made lakes. The largest, Lake of the Ozarks, is backed up behind Bagnell Dam, on the Osage River. This dam and Forsyth Dam, which makes Lake Taneycomo on the White River, are sites for hydroelectric-power.

Missouri is a rich agricultural state, with corn as the principal crop. Wheat, oats, hay, and soybeans are also important, as are fruits such as apples, peaches, strawberries, and watermelons. Missouri is still remembered for its mules, but other livestock and poultry are now more important. Long-staple cotton is an important crop in the Boot-heel and tobacco is important in the area north of Kansas City.

The two largest cities are across the state from each other. St. Louis is on the Mississippi at the eastern border of the state, near the point where the Missouri River enters the Mississippi. Kansas City is on the western border, where the Missouri enters the state. Both cities are river, railroad, airway, and highway transportation centers.

St. Louis, second oldest city in the state, has long been an important river port because of its strategic position on the Mississippi between the Ohio and the Missouri rivers. The city is proud of its cultural attainments, too. It boasts one of the oldest symphony orchestras in the nation and has one of the largest outdoor theaters, where summer opera is held. Among the many other attractions are a fine art museum, the Jefferson Memorial housing the Lindbergh trophies, and a beautiful botanical garden named the Jewel Box.

Kansas City and nearby Independence were important outfitting posts on the Santa Fe and Oregon trails. Kansas City is one of the nation's largest grain markets and meat-packing centers. Among her cultural attractions are the Philharmonic Orchestra, open-air Starlight Theater, William Rockhill Nelson Gallery of Art, and the Kansas City Museum.

Each of Missouri's two big cities has a big-league baseball team — the St. Louis Cardinals and the Kansas City Athletics.

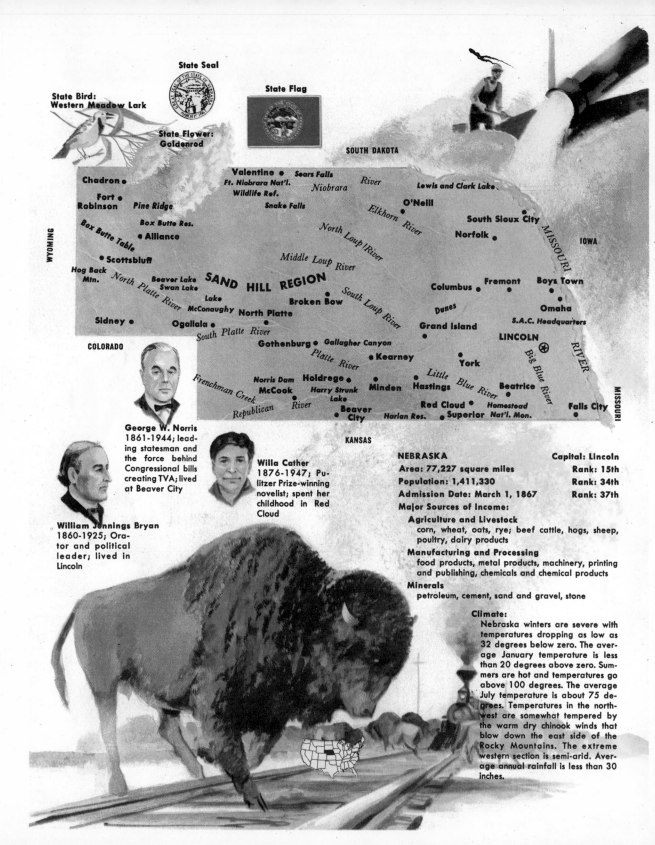

State Seal

State Bird:
Western Meadow Lark

State Flag

State Flower:
Goldenrod

SOUTH DAKOTA

WYOMING

Chadron

Fort
Robinson

Pine Ridge

Box Butte Table

Box Butte Res.
Alliance

Scottsbluff

Hog Back
Mtn.

North Platte River

Beaver Lake
Swan Lake

Lake
McConaughy

Sidney

Ogallala

South Platte River

COLORADO

Valentine   Sears Falls
Ft. Niobrara Nat'l.
Wildlife Ref.   Niobrara   River

Snake Falls

North Loup River

Middle Loup River

SAND HILL REGION

North Platte

Broken Bow

South Loup River

Gothenburg   Gallagher Canyon

Platte River   Kearney

Lewis and Clark Lake

O'Neill

Elkhorn River

South Sioux City

Norfolk

IOWA

MISSOURI

Columbus   Fremont   Boys Town

Dunes

Omaha

S.A.C. Headquarters

Grand Island

LINCOLN

York

Big Blue River

RIVER

MISSOURI

Norris Dam
McCook

Frenchman Creek

Republican   River

Holdrege

Harry Strunk
Lake

Minden

Beaver
City

Harlan Res.

Little   Blue River

Hastings

Red Cloud   Homestead
Superior   Nat'l. Mon.

Beatrice

Falls City

KANSAS

George W. Norris
1861-1944; lead-
ing statesman and
the force behind
Congressional bills
creating TVA; lived
at Beaver City

Willa Cather
1876-1947; Pu-
litzer Prize-winning
novelist; spent her
childhood in Red
Cloud

William Jennings Bryan
1860-1925; Ora-
tor and political
leader; lived in
Lincoln

NEBRASKA   Capital: Lincoln
Area: 77,227 square miles   Rank: 15th
Population: 1,411,330   Rank: 34th
Admission Date: March 1, 1867   Rank: 37th

Major Sources of Income:

Agriculture and Livestock
    corn, wheat, oats, rye; beef cattle, hogs, sheep,
    poultry, dairy products

Manufacturing and Processing
    food products, metal products, machinery, printing
    and publishing, chemicals and chemical products

Minerals
    petroleum, cement, sand and gravel, stone

Climate:
    Nebraska winters are severe with
    temperatures dropping as low as
    32 degrees below zero. The aver-
    age January temperature is less
    than 20 degrees above zero. Sum-
    mers are hot and temperatures go
    above 100 degrees. The average
    July temperature is about 75 de-
    grees. Temperatures in the north-
    west are somewhat tempered by
    the warm dry chinook winds that
    blow down the east side of the
    Rocky Mountains. The extreme
    western section is semi-arid. Aver-
    age annual rainfall is less than 30
    inches.

Settlers, with their eager eyes fixed on the wealth of California or the fertile land of the Oregon country, pressed westward along Nebraska's great Platte River. The Mormons crossed here on their way to build Salt Lake City; the pony express and the telegraph and the railroad all followed the Platte River through Nebraska. Forts were established along the route to protect the travelers. Occasionally pioneers, realizing that here was land as rich as could be found, stopped off along the way. Nebraska was made a territory by the Kansas-Nebraska Bill, but did not become a state until several years after the Civil War had ended.

Important Whens and Whats in the Making of Nebraska

1541 Coronado and his expedition enter the Nebraska region.

1700 French fur traders enter the land by way of the Missouri River about this time.

1803 Part of the Louisiana Purchase, Nebraska land becomes United States property.

1804 Lewis and Clark explore the eastern sections of the Nebraska area.

1812 Fort Lisa is built.

1854 The Territory of Nebraska is created by the Kansas-Nebraska Act.

1862 The Nebraska Homestead act is passed.

1863 At Omaha, ground is broken for the start of the Union Pacific Railroad.

1867 Nebraska is admitted to the Union as the 37th state.

Nebraska lies between South Dakota on the north and Kansas on the south. Its rivers, the Platte and its tributaries and the Niobrara in the north, flow into the Missouri, which forms the state's eastern boundary.

Nebraska's High Plains rise in the west to meet those of Wyoming and Colorado. In the extreme west, they form broken tablelands, with badlands in the northwest. East of the tablelands is a vast area of sand hills, grown over with prairie grass.

The eastern half of the state is largely loess hills and loess plains, with deep, fertile soil. Lowlands extend along the Platte River and the Missouri River. In the southeast corner are drift hills left by melting glaciers.

Nebraska is mainly an agricultural state, and one of the richest in the nation. Corn is the most important crop, although many others are grown, including wheat and other small grains, hay, vegetables, and fruit.

The great cattle ranches of Nebraska are in the west, mainly in the sand hills. Sheep, as well as cattle, are raised in the tablelands. Many of the cattle are sent to eastern Nebraska or to Iowa to be fattened on corn before going to market.

Although Nebraska has always been known as a prairie state, it does have some forest land, largely along the Missouri and Platte rivers and some of the Platte's tributaries, and in the Nebraska National Forest. The development of this forest, which is in two sections, one in northern Nebraska and the other in the center of the state, has aroused interest in tree planting, and Nebraska has become known as the "Tree Planters' State." Tree plantings, started by J. Sterling Morton at Nebraska City, developed into Arbor Day, which is now observed by most of the states in the Union. Mr. Morton's fifty-two-room home and arboretum are preserved in Arbor Lodge State Park.

Omaha, on the west bank of the Missouri River, is noted as a railroad and meat-packing center. Nearby is the famous Boys Town, founded by the late Father Edward J. Flanagan as a home for friendless boys.

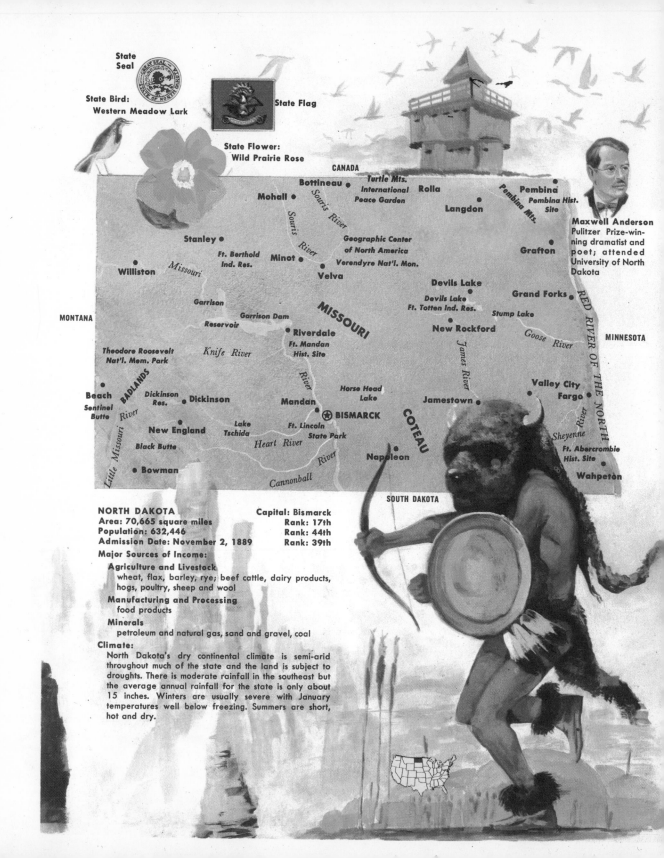

State Seal

State Bird: Western Meadow Lark

State Flag

State Flower: Wild Prairie Rose

CANADA

Bottineau
Mohall
Turtle Mts.
International
Peace Garden
Rolla
Langdon
Pembina
Pembina Hist. Site
Pembina Mts.

Stanley
Ft. Berthold Ind. Res.
Minot
Geographic Center of North America
Verendyre Nat'l. Mon.
Velva
Grafton

Williston
Missouri
Souris River

Devils Lake
Devils Lake
Ft. Totten Ind. Res.
Stump Lake
Grand Forks

Maxwell Anderson Pulitzer Prize-winning dramatist and poet; attended University of North Dakota

MONTANA

Garrison
Garrison Dam
Reservoir
Riverdale
Ft. Mandan Hist. Site
MISSOURI
New Rockford
Goose River

Theodore Roosevelt Nat'l. Mem. Park
Knife River
River

MINNESOTA

RED RIVER OF THE NORTH

BADLANDS
Beach
Sentinel Butte
Dickinson Res.
Dickinson
Mandan
Horse Head Lake
Jamestown
Valley City
Fargo
James River

New England
Lake Tschida
Ft. Lincoln State Park
BISMARCK
COTEAU
Sheyenne River
Ft. Abercrombie Hist. Site

Black Butte
Heart River
Napoleon
Wahpeton

Little Missouri River
Bowman
Cannonball River

SOUTH DAKOTA

NORTH DAKOTA
Area: 70,665 square miles
Population: 632,446
Admission Date: November 2, 1889

Capital: Bismarck
Rank: 17th
Rank: 44th
Rank: 39th

Major Sources of Income:

Agriculture and Livestock
wheat, flax, barley, rye; beef cattle, dairy products, hogs, poultry, sheep and wool

Manufacturing and Processing
food products

Minerals
petroleum and natural gas, sand and gravel, coal

Climate:
North Dakota's dry continental climate is semi-arid throughout much of the state and the land is subject to droughts. There is moderate rainfall in the southeast but the average annual rainfall for the state is only about 15 inches. Winters are usually severe with January temperatures well below freezing. Summers are short, hot and dry.

North Dakota, Theodore Roosevelt's adopted state, borders Canada on the north and shares with her the International Peace Garden, commemorating almost 150 years of peace between Canada and the United States. From the fertile valley of the Red River of the North, on the eastern border, to the western badlands, the state holds many things of interest to the rest of the nation.

Important Whens and Whats in the Making of North Dakota

1738-1740	Pierre de la Vérendrye and other French-Canadians explore North Dakota lands.
1797	A trading post is established on the Pembina River.
1803	Part of the Louisiana Purchase, the region becomes United States property.
1804	Lewis and Clark, exploring their way west, establish Fort Mandan.
1861	North Dakota land, and South Dakota and part of Montana and Wyoming make up the Dakota Territory.
1862-1866	Sioux Indian Wars.
1876	General Custer and his troops start from Fort Abraham Lincoln for the battle of the Little Bighorn.
1881	The Northern Pacific Railroad reaches across North Dakota.
1889	North Dakota becomes a separate state and is admitted to the Union along with South Dakota.

Devils Lake, on the northeast border of the Fort Totten Indian Reservation, is the second-largest salt lake in the United States, and there are numerous other natural and man-made lakes in the eastern half of the state. Garrison Reservoir, in the western half, absorbs a large part of the Fort Berthold Indian Reservation. Mandan, on the Missouri River south of the reservoir, is surrounded by ancient Indian villages and historic forts.

North Dakota's land follows the general pattern of the western Plains States, sloping up from lower land on the east to an elevation of several thousand feet on the western border. The eastern part is a drift plain, with deep soil, boulders, and small hills left by melting glaciers.

The state is mainly agricultural, with wheat as its leading agricultural product; it competes with Kansas for the title of the nation's "breadbasket." Other important crops are barley and flax. Corn is grown in the southeastern section of the state, and hogs and poultry are raised here, too. Cattle and sheep are raised in all parts of the state.

Dust storms in the 1930's brought great hardship to the farmers in the western section, but more favorable conditions developed in later years, and the discovery of oil in the Williston Basin hastened recovery. There are valuable coal deposits in the western section, also, with lignite strip mines in the Minot area.

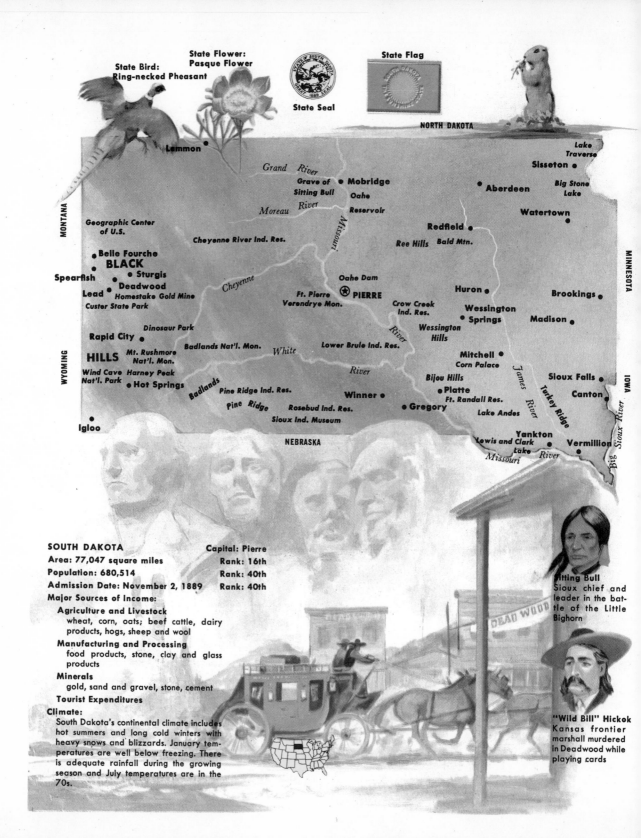

State Bird:
Ring-necked Pheasant

State Flower:
Pasque Flower

State Seal

State Flag

NORTH DAKOTA

MONTANA

Lemmon

Grand River

Grave of Sitting Bull

Mobridge

Oahe

Moreau River

Oahe Reservoir

Lake Traverse

Sisseton

Big Stone Lake

Aberdeen

Watertown

Geographic Center of U.S.

Cheyenne River Ind. Res.

Redfield

Ree Hills   Bald Mtn.

Belle Fourche
BLACK

Spearfish   Sturgis

Lead   Deadwood
Homestake Gold Mine

Custer State Park

Cheyenne

Oahe Dam

Ft. Pierre
Verendrye Mon.   PIERRE

Crow Creek Ind. Res.

Huron

Wessington Springs

Brookings

Madison

MINNESOTA

Dinosaur Park

Rapid City

HILLS   Mt. Rushmore Nat'l. Mon.

Badlands Nat'l. Mon.

White

Wessington Hills

Lower Brule Ind. Res.

River

Mitchell
Corn Palace

Sioux Falls

WYOMING

Wind Cave Nat'l. Park   Harney Peak

Hot Springs

Badlands

Pine Ridge Ind. Res.

Pine Ridge

River

Winner

Rosebud Ind. Res.

Sioux Ind. Museum

Bijou Hills

Platte
Ft. Randall Res.

Gregory

Lake Andes

James River

Turkey Ridge

Canton

IOWA

Igloo

NEBRASKA

Yankton

Lewis and Clark Lake

Lewis and Clark Lake

Missouri   River

Vermillion

Big Sioux River

SOUTH DAKOTA

Area: 77,047 square miles   Capital: Pierre
Population: 680,514   Rank: 16th
Admission Date: November 2, 1889   Rank: 40th
   Rank: 40th

Major Sources of Income:

Agriculture and Livestock
   wheat, corn, oats; beef cattle, dairy products, hogs, sheep and wool

Manufacturing and Processing
   food products, stone, clay and glass products

Minerals
   gold, sand and gravel, stone, cement

Tourist Expenditures

Climate:
South Dakota's continental climate includes hot summers and long cold winters with heavy snows and blizzards. January temperatures are well below freezing. There is adequate rainfall during the growing season and July temperatures are in the 70s.

DEAD WOOD

Sitting Bull
Sioux chief and leader in the battle of the Little Bighorn

"Wild Bill" Hickok
Kansas frontier marshall murdered in Deadwood while playing cards

South Dakota has long been a favorite state with visitors because of its highly scenic Badlands and Black Hills, which are the source, also, of most of the mineral wealth of the state. The string of large, man-made lakes on the Missouri River and the many natural lakes in northeastern South Dakota have added to the state's attractions. Water sports of all sorts, as well as fine fishing, are available in most of the lakes.

Important Whens and Whats in the Making of South Dakota

1743   The sons of Pierre de la Vérandrye, in search of a route to the Pacific, are the first white men to discover the region.

1803   Part of the Louisiana Purchase, the land becomes United States property.

1804   Lewis and Clark explore the South Dakota region.

1817   Bad River, the first permanent settlement, is founded by Americans.

1860   At Bon Homme, the first schoolhouse is built.

1861   The Dakota Territory, including South Dakota land, is created.

1874   General Custer discovers gold in the Black Hills.

1889   Along with North Dakota, South Dakota enters the Union as a separate state.

The eastern part of the state is a drift plain, with rich soil, boulders, moraines, and numerous small lakes scooped out by the glaciers. The western section is a high plain or tableland, with the Badlands and the Black Hills, which are really mountains, in the southwest corner. The Black Hills are so named because they are covered with thick evergreen forests which, from a distance, look black.

South Dakota is largely agricultural, with crops and dairying in the east and beef cattle and sheep in the west. Like North Dakota, it has been plagued with drought and dust storms. In the central section, deep wells have helped to relieve the water shortage. Much of the state is set aside in Indian reservations.

Pheasant hunting is popular in the eastern part of the state, and elk, deer, and antelope are in the Black Hills and other sections of the west. Some good places to see these animals, and buffalo as well, are in the Wind Cave National Park and Custer State Park. Another interesting sight in the state park is Needles Highway, with its towering pinnacles of rock. It's fun to drive to the Mount Rushmore Memorial, too, over switchbacks with breathtaking views and across "pigtail" bridges that curl back over themselves. Beautiful views of the "faces" of the Memorial can be seen along the way; an especially fine view is framed by the mouth of a tunnel.

Near the Badlands, on the Rosebud Indian Reservation, an interesting park is maintained in Crazy Horse Canyon by the Rosebud Sioux tribe. In the scenic setting of this canyon you can ride Indian ponies on real Sioux trails, watch Sioux dances, and see Indian villages, where Sioux women dry meat, and make beaded clothing. The Sioux Indian Museum at St. Francis is considered one of the finest in the country.

Glossary

arboretum (är′bo̊ rē′tŭm) a place where trees and shrubs are cultivated for scientific or educational purposes.

artifact (är′tĭ făkt) a product of human workmanship, especially of primitive skill.

badlands (băd′lăndz′) regions where erosion has carved soft rocks into detailed and fantastic shapes and where vegetation is scanty.

barter (bär′tēr) to trade or exchange goods or services for other products or services without the use of money.

bluff (blŭf) a part of mountains or hills which rises steeply with a broad, flat or rounded front, as a coast or at the edge of some rivers.

bog (bŏg) an area filled with decayed moss and other vegetable matter; wet spongy ground.

botanical (bo̊ tăn′ĭ kăl) having to do with plants; relating to the study of plants.

butte (būt) an isolated hill or small mountain with very steep sides.

cairn (kârn) a heap of stones raised as a memorial or a landmark.

culture (kŭl′tŭr) 1. a particular stage in the development of a civilization; 2. the characteristic features of such a stage.

diorama (dī′o̊ rä′må) 1. a method of representing a scene in which a picture is seen from a distance through an opening; 2. a small scenic representation using small three-dimensional figures in a lighted setting.

fossil (fŏs′ĭl) any impression or trace, of an animal or plant of the past, which has been preserved in the earth's crust.

glaciated (glā′shĭ āt′d) the action or effect of a glacier—as erosion and relocated earth.

glacier (glā′shēr) a field or body of ice which moves slowly down a valley from above.

gristmill (grĭst′mĭl) a mill for grinding grain.

hydroelectric-power (hĭ′dro̊ e̊ lĕk′trĭc) the production of electricity by water power or steam.

immigrant (ĭm′ĭ grănt) one who comes into a country of which he is not a native, for permanent residence.

loess (lō′ĕs; lûs) a deposit of yellowish-brown soft, fine dirt covering areas in North America, Europe, and Asia.

mammoth (măm′ŭth) 1. an elephant no longer living, known by its large teeth and cement-like material between the teeth; 2. referring to size—being very large.

mastodon (măs′tȯ dŏn) an elephant-like animal which is no longer living, differing from a mammoth in the molar teeth.

moraine (mȯ rān′) an accumulation or collection of earth, stones, and debris deposited by a glacier.

nomadic (nȯ măd′ĭk) as a group of people, or tribe, that has no fixed location; wandering from place to place.

peccary (pĕk′ȧ rĭ) an American pig-like mammal about three feet long and grizzled, with a distinct white collar or all black with whitish cheeks.

pinnacle (pĭn′ȧ k′l) a tall, slender, pointed mass, especially a lofty peak.

potholes (pŏt′hōlz′) small marshes, usually with a small pond or pool at the center.

reservoir (rĕz′ẽr vwôr) a place where water is collected and kept for use when needed.

roller-gate dam (rōl′ẽr gāt dăm) a dam or the structure of a dam whose gate is raised as it forms a continuous roll at the upper end.

sect (sĕkt) 1. a group having in common a leader or a distinctive doctrine or belief; 2. a group holding similar views, or ideas.

semi-arid (sĕm′ĭ′ăr′ĭd) partially dry; with little moisture.

switchback (swĭch′băk′) a road which zigzags in mountainous regions; the arrangement of zigzags in railroad tracks for surmounting the rise of a steep hill.

tableland (tā′b′l lănd) a broad elevated plateau with steep cliff-like sides leading down to the adjoining lowlands or sea.

Grateful acknowledgment is made to the following for the helpful information and materials furnished by them used in the preparation of this book:

United States Department of the Interior, National Park Service; particularly Wind Cave National Park and its management.

United States Department of Commerce, Bureau of the Census, Field Services, Chicago, Illinois.

Iowa Development Commission.

Kansas Industrial Development Commission.

Missouri Resources and Development Commission.

Nebraska Division of Nebraska Resources.

North Dakota State Library Commission.

State of South Dakota Department of Highways.

International Visual Educational Services, Inc., Chicago, Illinois.

Index

A COMMENTARY

ON THE GENERAL PROLOGUE TO

THE CANTERBURY TALES

THE MACMILLAN COMPANY
NEW YORK · CHICAGO
DALLAS · ATLANTA · SAN FRANCISCO
LONDON · MANILA

IN CANADA
BRETT-MACMILLAN LTD.
GALT, ONTARIO